D0475571

MONTANA BRANCH
Santa Monica Public Library

MAR - - 2017

What sails?
What flies?

Those . . . these

Down low

nearby

far off . . .

up high

Who listens?
Who looks?

Who hears?
Who sees?

all ears,

by Richard Jackson

all eyes

illustrated by Katherine Tillotson

A CAITLYN DLOUHY BOOK

Atheneum Books for Young Readers
New York London Toronto Sydney New Delhi

atheneum

ATHENEUM BOOKS FOR YOUNG READERS
An imprint of Simon & Schuster Children's Publishing Division
1230 Avenue of the Americas, New York, New York 10020
Text copyright © 2017 by Richard Jackson
Illustrations copyright © 2017 by Katherine Tillotson
All rights reserved, including the right of reproduction in whole
or in part in any form.
ATHENEUM BOOKS FOR YOUNG READERS is a registered trademark of
Simon & Schuster, Inc.
Atheneum logo is a trademark of Simon & Schuster, Inc.
For information about special discounts for bulk purchases, please
contact Simon & Schuster Special Sales at 1-866-506-1949 or
business@simonandschuster.com.
The Simon & Schuster Speakers Bureau can bring authors to your
live event. For more information or to book an event, contact the
Simon & Schuster Speakers Bureau at 1-866-248-3049 or visit our
website at www.simonspeakers.com.
Book design by Ann Bobco and Katherine Tillotson
The text for this book was set in Grit Primer.
The illustrations for this book were rendered using a combination of
watercolor and digital techniques.
Manufactured in China
1216 SCP
First Edition
10 9 8 7 6 5 4 3 2 1
Library of Congress Cataloging-in-Publication Data
Jackson, Richard, 1935–
All ears, all eyes / Richard Jackson ; illustrated by Katherine Tillotson. —
First edition.
pages cm
Summary: As darkness falls in the forest, animals hoot, chirp, whirr, and
bark, lulling drowsy children to sleep.
ISBN 978-1-4814-1571-2 (hardcover)
ISBN 978-1-4814-1572-9 (eBook)
[1. Stories in rhyme. 2. Animal sounds—Fiction. 3. Forest animals—
Fiction. 4. Bedtime—Fiction.] I. Tillotson, Katherine, illustrator. II. Title.
PZ8.3.J1357Al 2015
[E]—dc23   2014003384

To Nancy
with my love

To Adam, Tess, and the memory of Sam,
and to Kelsey and Alexander
with our love

—R. J.

To Bob, with love

—K. T.

An owl hoots
in our dim-dimming woods.

Who-who

Raccoon at sundown, romping
Another, her brother, he's chomping

What scoots
between roots?

All ears,
a bat flies,
wings whirring

Deer here

as light falls
and night rises.

Flying squirrels . . .
could be boys
could be girls

What surprises?
What sings?

Crick-crick-crickets **chirring** *in the thick-thick-thickets*

Whoo-whoo

A fox flees,
bark-bark-barking!

Chipmunks
stirring, harking
on tree trunks

One mouse,
two.

Me, you . . .
all eyes.

Wink,

and there are fireflies

everywhere,

flicking . . . flashing

in mid air

Fox, mouse, owl, bat,
this and that
(was that a cat?)
in our deep, dark woods.

There!

Shhh

vole
hole

See it?
Hear it?

Tree frog agog,
scree-scree-screeing on a log-og-og

Owl's call
Bat's whirr
Frog's peep
Cricket's chirr
Fox's bark
blur...

Moon pales
among trees.

Comes a breeze—
they bend and bow—

and behind these,
beyond those

deep
in the dark,
near to brimming now,

Nature's ark
glows,
gathers
tiny and tall,
splendid and small

and sails

us all

to sleep.